veghsg

PLAYGROUNDS
BY GAIL GIBBONS

Holiday House
New York

For Simone Scovel

Library of Congress Cataloging in Publication Data

Gibbons, Gail.
  Playgrounds.

  Summary: Introduces the various types of playground
equipment, including swings, slides, and sandboxes, as
well as games and toys that may be enjoyed at the
playground.
  1. Playgrounds—Juvenile literature. [1. Playgrounds.
2. Play]   I. Title.
GV423.G52   1985   790'.06'8   84-19285
ISBN 0-8234-0553-2

A playground is a place to play.
There are many different things to use.

There are different kinds of swings.

swing

sling swing

baby swing

glide ride

Some are very simple.

tire swing

rope swing

pony swing

double glide ride

lawn swing

Up on a swing everything looks different.

It feels windy, too.

There are seesaws.

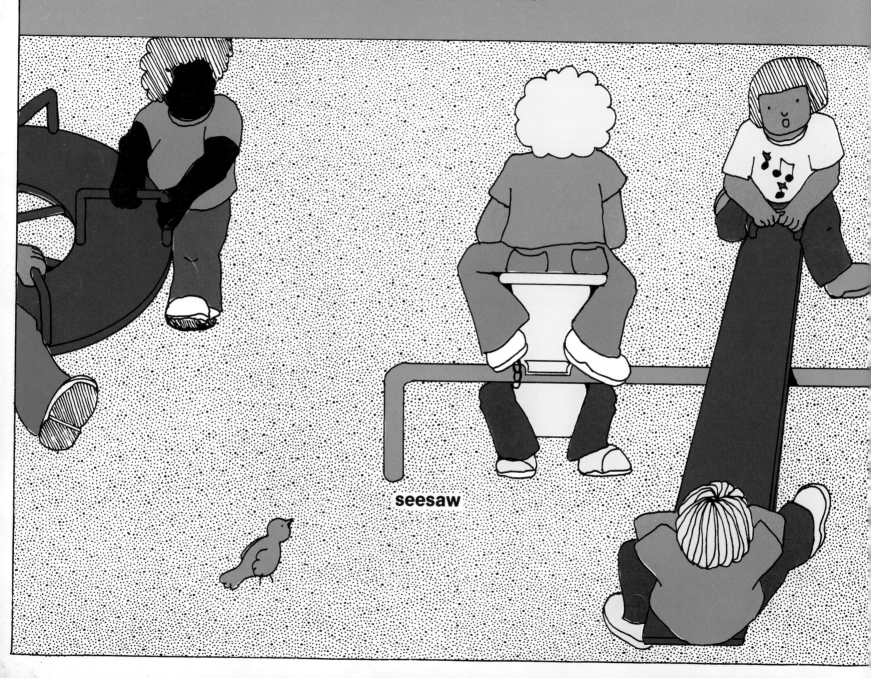

seesaw

They go up . . .   up . . .
          and down . . .   and down.

It's fun to play in a sandbox . . .

sandbox

and make sand cakes and build castles.

sifter

mold

shovel

sand pail

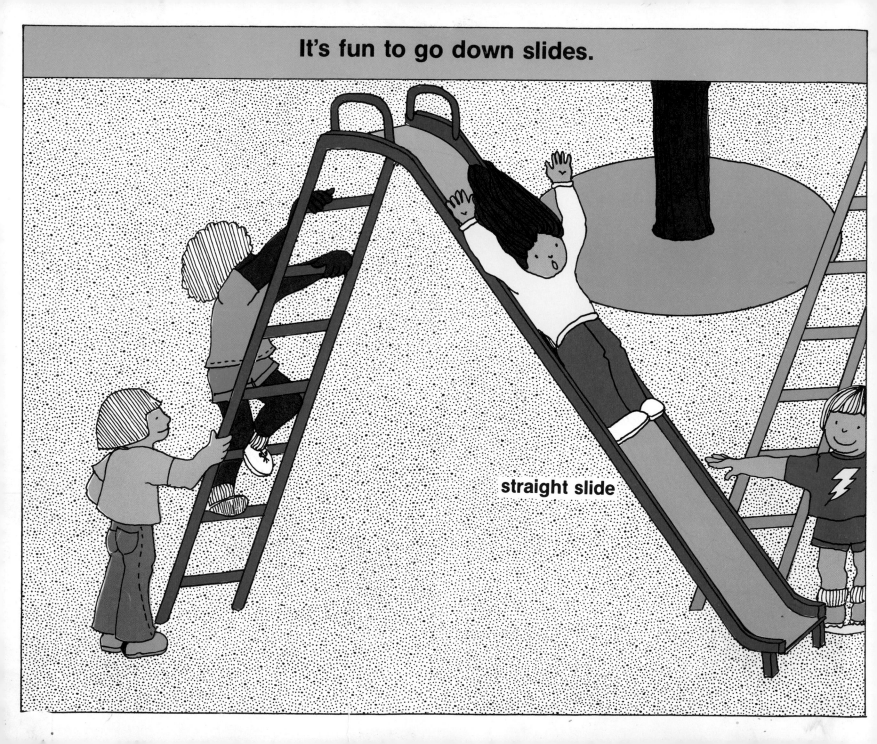

It's fun to go down slides.

straight slide

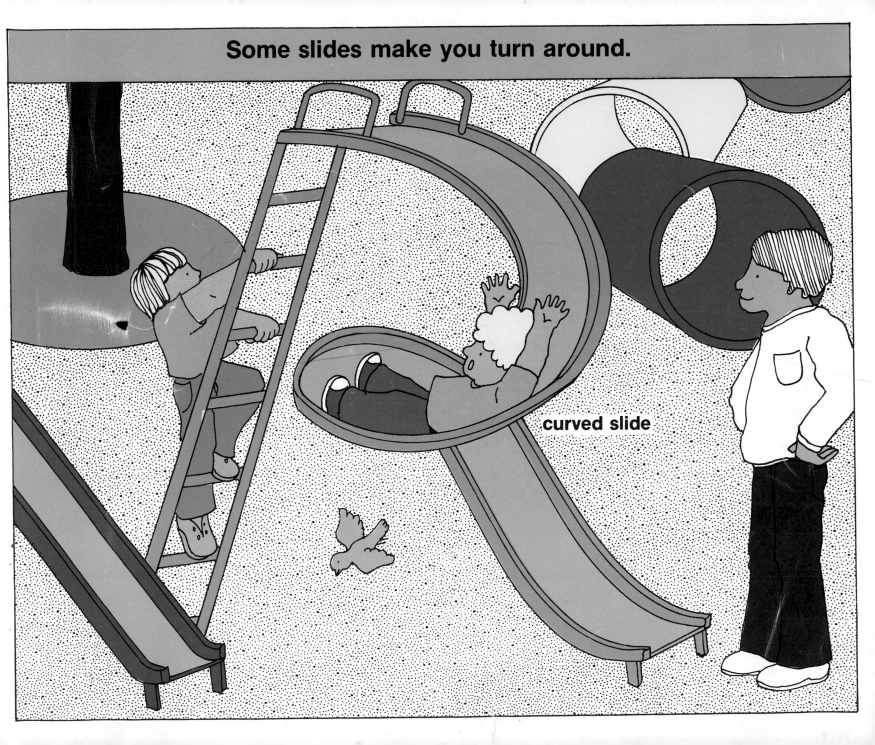

Some slides make you turn around.

curved slide

There are ground games to play.
Sometimes a ball is used.

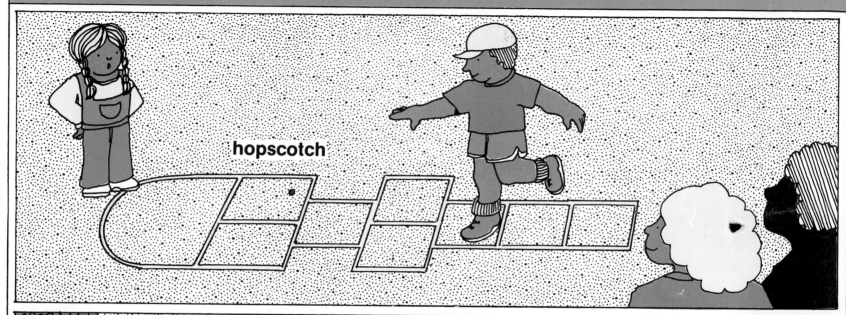

hopscotch

tag ball circle

A merry-go-round spins round and round.
It goes s l o w ... *fast* ... s l o w.

merry-go-round

jungle gym

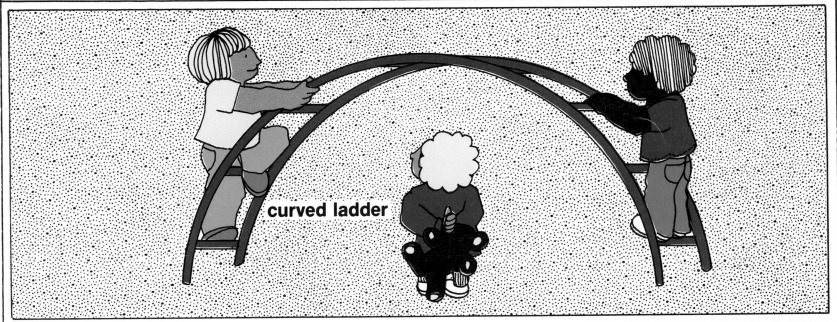

curved ladder

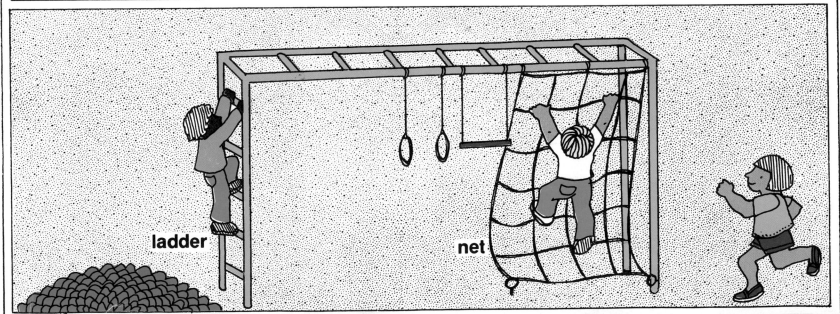

ladder

net

and crawl through . . .

tube tunnels

tire obstacle course

There are trapezes and rings . . .

rings

trapeze

and ladders, too.

hand-over-hand ladder

Also, it's fun to bring things to use at the playground.

jacks

bubbles

ball

jump rope

tricycle

Yo-Yo

skateboard

roller skates

marbles

sprinkler

or play in a wading pool.

wading pool